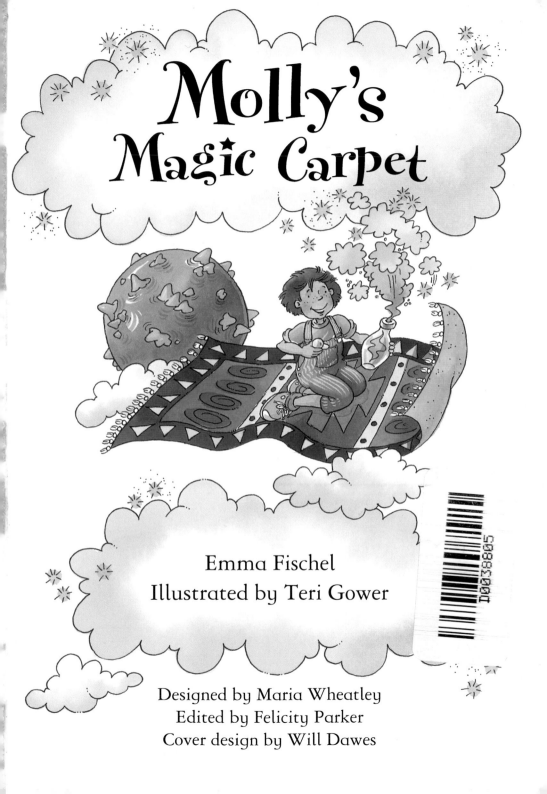

Molly's Magic Carpet

Emma Fischel
Illustrated by Teri Gower

Designed by Maria Wheatley
Edited by Felicity Parker
Cover design by Will Dawes

Contents

Meet Molly

This is Molly. There is an amazing adventure waiting for her. Turn the page to find out more!

Look out for the clues! If you get stuck, there are answers on pages 31 and 32.

The mysterious voice

"CHARGE!" shouted Molly. Today, she was a knight, off to tame a dragon. But...

CRASH!

BANG!

WALLOP!

"Ouch," said Molly, rubbing her bottom. "That hurt."

"Well, look where you're going next time," grumbled a little voice.

Molly jumped. Who had said that?

"Get your muddy feet off my back.
You'll get my pattern dirty."

Molly looked around. She couldn't see
anyone, but something had spoken. It must
be something magic.

What do you think it is?

Up, up and away!

"You're a magic carpet!" Molly gasped, nearly toppling over.

"Almost," sighed the carpet. "But I can't be a real magic carpet until I do something brave. Time's running out. Soon I'll just be an *ordinary* carpet – no voice, no flying, nothing!"

"Poor carpet," said Molly. "I'll help you find something brave to do."

"You will?" the carpet said happily. "Hop on!"

"Let's go to the big blue planet. Hold on tight!"

Can you help them find their way to the big blue planet?

Wonderworld

"This is Wonderworld," the carpet said when they arrived. "We're sure to find adventure here."

"Wow," said Molly. "What are all those places called?"

"There's Cloudworld, Spookville, One Mountain Island, Topsy-turvydom and Monsterland" the carpet replied.

Which island do you think is which?

9

Rocky ride

Suddenly, the carpet gasped. "I'm running out of flying magic."
Molly and the carpet were spinning towards the sea. They landed on a rock with a THUD.

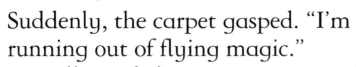

"We'll have to hop from rock to rock to the beach," said Molly.
"I'm far too tired," sniffed the carpet. "You'll have to carry me."
Then they heard a shout.

Can you find a safe way to the beach?

Safely ashore

"Made it," panted Molly, flopping down onto the sand.

"Unroll me, please," said a muffled voice.

"Wow! Is that a talking carpet?" asked the boy on the beach. "I'm Frank and this is my rabbit. Did you really fly to Wonderworld?"

"All the way," said Molly proudly. "I'm hungry now though."

"Let's fly to the Candy Café and have something to eat," said Frank.

"What does it look like?" asked the carpet.

"It's blue and has parasols outside," Frank replied.

Can you spot the Candy Café?

Carnival chaos

It was carnival day in the town. Molly was enjoying the fun when... DONG! A huge gong boomed out.

Suddenly, everyone stopped moving... everyone except Molly. They all froze to the spot like statues.

What was going on? Then... DONG!

Everyone sprang back into life. "What happened?" Molly asked Frank. But he didn't answer. He was too busy looking for his rabbit.

Can you see Frank's rabbit in this picture?

Magic mix-up

"That happens a lot," sighed Frank. "It's all because of Mort the magician."

He began to explain...

"Mort lives in a castle on top of the mountain.

One day he sent the village an invitation.

I have a brilliant new spell! Come and see it at 2 o'clock sharp. Love from Mort

The whole town came to see Mort do his magic.

This spell will turn vegetables into ice cream!

I open the jar...

and hey presto!

But something was wrong.
Mort started to change...

We thought it was funny,
but Mort was furious."

You'll be
sorry you
laughed at me!

Can you spot all the
changes to Mort?

Molly has a plan

"He was so angry, he made a new spell," said Frank. "Now any time he opens his spell jar, the blue clouds float out and we all freeze to the spot."

"Can't you stop him somehow?" asked Molly.

"Only by taking the jar with the blue clouds in," said Frank. "But we can't get up the mountain as he's covered it in sticky toffee. We've tried everything."

Candy Café - Ices, jellies and lots more

"Mort must use magic to get to the castle," Molly said thoughtfully. "So can we. Let's fly there on the carpet!"

The carpet didn't like the sound of this and flew off to hide.

Where is the carpet hiding?

Flying high

"This is your big chance to do something brave," said Molly, hugging the carpet.

"I don't feel very brave," it said in a wobbly voice. "But I do want to be a real magic carpet. So, let's go!"

"To the top of the mountain!" shouted Molly, and jumped onto the carpet.

Up and up they flew. The side of the mountain grew steeper and steeper. The clouds rushed past. And all the while the castle grew closer and closer.

At last they reached the castle.
Three magic birds flew up to Molly.
They seemed to be trying to help her.

Can you find the secret passage?

Underground

The dungeon was slimy and dark. The carpet started shaking like a leaf.

"Which way do we go?" Molly gulped. Then she saw a map.

Can you find the way in?

Way into castle

WARNING: WATCH OUT FOR FIERY
DRAGONS AND SLITHERING SNAKES!

Dungeon
entrance

You
are
here.

Surprises in Store

"We have to find the spell jar," whispered Molly. They searched high and low...

behind big doors...

stiff doors...

and creaky doors.

There was only one place left to look – the tower.

At the top of the tower, not one...
not two... but three Morts were waiting.
"Surprise!" they chortled. "You must
solve our riddle to find the real Mort."

The man you seek is one of us three
But not in spots or stripes is he.
The one with yellow stars you see
Is he you want, you see he's me.

Can you solve the riddle
and spot the real Mort?

The spell jar

Two of the magicians vanished. Molly and the carpet rushed past and bolted the door.

"You won't keep me out forever!" cried Mort. He began mumbling a spell to unlock the door.

"Quick, look for a jar with blue clouds in it," said Molly.

Can you find the spell jar?

A smashing time

"Found it!" shrieked Molly. "Let's go!" She leaped onto the carpet and they soared out of the window.

Molly flung the spell jar up in the air. Down it fell, faster and faster, until...

SMASH! A puffy blue cloud drifted away into the sky.

"Good riddance!" shouted the carpet. "Hold on tight, Molly. It's a long way down."

They whooshed through the clouds.

They chased shooting stars...

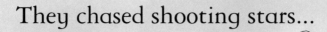

surfed on the breeze...

and raced waterfalls down the mountainside.

Then Molly saw something. It was a tree she had noticed before, that told her they were nearly back in the town.

Which tree does Molly recognize?

Homeward bound

"See?" Molly said to the carpet. "You *are* brave after all."

Then she noticed something – a golden label... "You've done it!" she cried, and hugged the carpet tightly. "You're a real magic carpet now!"

"Fancy that!" it said, curling up at one corner with pleasure.

It was time to go home. "I wish our adventure didn't have to end," Molly sighed.

The carpet laughed. "Who knows where we'll go next time?"

Genuine Magic Carpet